Sisters Learn Traditional Foods

The Oolichan Fish

Samantha Beynon
Illustrated by Lucy Trimble

Dedication

SB – Rae, Blake and Jamie our forever and always

LT – My darlings Kwikwenaw, Miya, and all my relations.

Ways to spell Oolichan

Eulachon Ooligan Hooligan Candlefish

Nisga'a Language

oolichans – saak – s[aa]k

eat oolichans (to) – x̱saak – x̱[saa]k

fish – Hoon – [hoo]n

Grandmother – nits'iits' – ni[ts'ii]ts'

Grandfather – niye'e – ni[ye'e]

playmate/partner/brother/sister – sdik'eekw – sdi[k'ee]kw

brother/sister – gimxdi – gimx[di]

sisters/brothers – gimxditkws – gimx[ditkws]

sister (a female)'s – hlgiikw hl[gii]kw

little girl – hlgutk'ihlgum hanaḵ' – hlgut[k'ihl]gum ha[naḵ']

big/great – ẃii – ẃii

Big Sister (a female) – ẃii hlgiikw

year-old dry food (i.e., salted fish, grease) oolichan – aguus – a[guu]s

greasy/ fatty (food, to be) – ṁ ax̱t'ilx – [ṁ ax̱[t'il]x

pulp from cooked oolichan, used as putty on bent storage boxes to prevent leaking when storing grease – anaaya saak – an[aa]ya [saa]k

camp for processing oolichans – anjog̱ am sisaak – anjog̱ am si[saak]

In the month of February, the observation of the crescent moon and the star aligning in the shape of a spoon when it is full. This signifies a bountiful harvest year – Hobiyee – [Ho]biyee

catch and process oolichans (to) – sisaak – si[saa]k

Source: First Peoples' Cultural Council (FPCC). "Nisga'a." *FirstVoices*, 10 Feb. 2021, www.firstvoices.com/explore/FV/sections/Data/Nisga'a/Nisga'a/Nisga'a.

As the two sisters fell asleep,

they dreamt vividly of the rich traditional foods their Grandmother and Grandfather would feed them all year round. The sisters dreamt mostly of the oolichan fish, which is a very important dish to many of their people. The sisters were lucky to have their grandparents, as both were important Elders within the community who held many Sacred Oral Traditions that had been passed down to them from their ancestors.

Little Sister was always the first one to wake up in their grandparents' home. She woke up eager, excited, and wanting to learn more about the oolichan fish, as her dreams had motivated her to grow her knowledge. Little Sister knew it was near the end of winter, coming to the beginning of spring, and this was a very special season for her family, friends, and surrounding communities. As soon as she awoke, she asked Grandmother for all the knowledge and history surrounding the oolichan fish.

Grandmother was honoured that Little Sister had asked her for this knowledge. The importance of the oolichan fish had been passed down for many generations, and it was very important to Grandmother that she passed it down to the next.

Grandfather made tea, and the four of them sat in the living room, elated to hear Grandmother's stories.

The sisters sat on the floor by Grandmother's feet and waited patiently for Grandmother to begin.

Grandmother closed her eyes and reflected on the years of wealth she retained about the oolichan fish. As she finished thinking, she took a deep breath and a sip of tea, then she felt that she was ready to pass the traditional stories and learnings on to her beloved granddaughters.

Grandmother started by acknowledging

and thanking her ancestors for all their hard work and knowledge that had been passed down to her. She felt extreme gratitude that she could pass on this knowledge. Grandmother had been waiting for this moment for a very long time, so she felt very emotional in a happy, heartfelt way.

Grandmother said,

"Oolichan harvesting started thousands of years ago for our people. The oolichan fish is very important, as it is the first fish to return to the river after winter. Oolichans are rich in vitamins, and fatty enough for our people to thrive and stay healthy for many generations. When I was a young girl, the Elders told me that the oolichan is called our saviour fish. I did not understand why they would say this, but now I do. The oolichan fish has kept our people alive for thousands of years as it is very fatty, is rich in vitamins, and is a good source of protein. This little fish is amazing, you see."

12

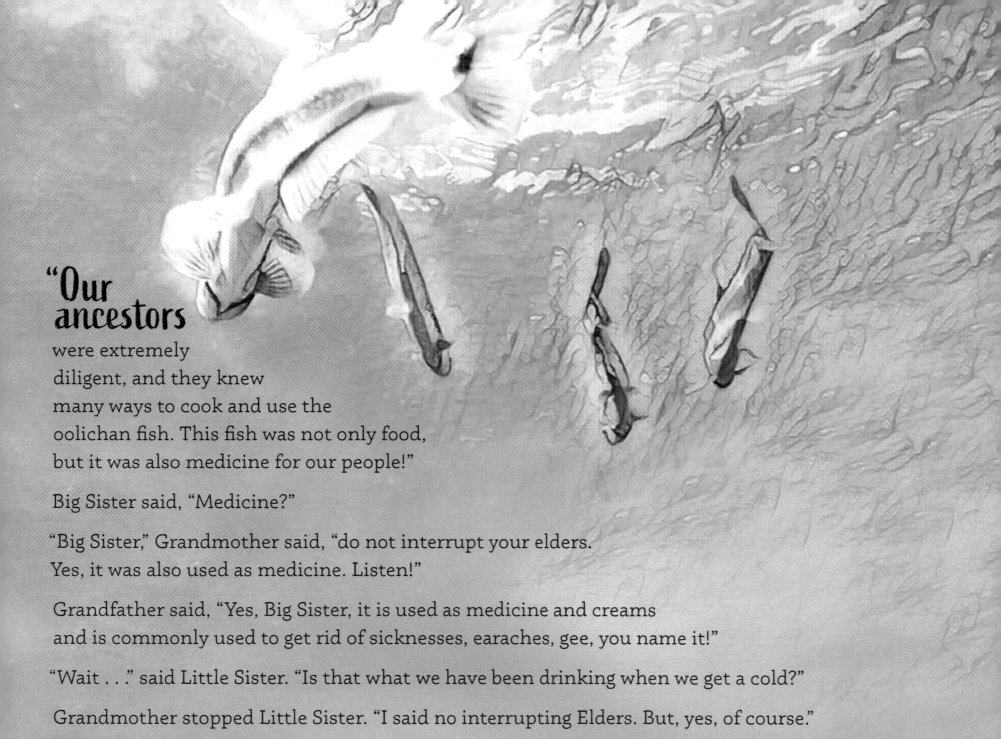

"Our ancestors were extremely diligent, and they knew many ways to cook and use the oolichan fish. This fish was not only food, but it was also medicine for our people!"

Big Sister said, "Medicine?"

"Big Sister," Grandmother said, "do not interrupt your elders. Yes, it was also used as medicine. Listen!"

Grandfather said, "Yes, Big Sister, it is used as medicine and creams and is commonly used to get rid of sicknesses, earaches, gee, you name it!"

"Wait . . ." said Little Sister. "Is that what we have been drinking when we get a cold?"

Grandmother stopped Little Sister. "I said no interrupting Elders. But, yes, of course."

14

"As I was saying . . ."
Grandmother said,

"the oolichan fish is used and cooked in many different ways. Our people eat oolichans fresh by frying, baking, boiling, sun drying, or smoking, which allows us to preserve and use them all year around. Because this fish is so oily, we can make a wick and use it as a candle.

"But most importantly, the arrival of spawning oolichans signifies a new year for our Nisga'a people where we celebrate Hoobiyee. Hoobiyee, Nisga'a new year, is also very important, as is signifies the last crescent of the moon and the beginning of the new year for our people."

15

Grandmother
said,

"This fish is so fatty we are able to have liquid gold. And when I say liquid gold, I mean oolichan grease. Oolichans are stored in wide cedar bent boxes until the grease separates and rises to the top of the boxes. The layer of grease is skimmed, then stored away to be used throughout the year or traded with other surrounding communities."

"This little fish is also very important to many other nations and communities," said Grandmother. "Even within our community, the oolichan fish may have different traditions and ways of cooking and spelling it. The ways of the oolichan differ from house to house, but the one thing everyone has in common is the joy this little fish brings us all."

After Grandmother finished passing on her teachings and stories, both of the sisters felt extreme appreciation to have learned the valuable learnings about the oolichan fish. Both sisters hugged Grandmother and Grandfather and thanked them for all their valued teachings. Both sisters grew up learning the importance of the oolichan; however, both learned way more, which made them appreciate their heritage and traditional foods and understand just how

valuable and important the oolichan fish is.

Grandmother had a big surprise she had been keeping. She informed the sisters and Grandfather that their auntie would be dropping off fresh oolichans for lunchtime! Both sisters were salivating, thinking of the rich, oily fish that they had waited so long for.

When the fish arrived, Grandmother fried the oolichans, paired with boiled potatoes, and the four of them enjoyed a meaningful lunch full of history, laughter, and love.

After they had finished their lunch, Little Sister whispered in Big Sister's ear, "Let's ask for fish, rice, and oolichan grease for dinner."

THE END.

History of the Oolichan Fish

AT A GLANCE

For thousands of years, the Nisga'a people have harvested oolichan from K̲'alii- Aksim Lisims, the Nass River. It is their saviour fish, its arrival signaling winter is over and the season of harvest has begun.

The devastating collapse of oolichan stocks across the coast of British Columbia has impacted First Nations' culture and access to traditional foods. In 2011, when the K̲'alii- Aksim Lisims oolichan was assessed as "threatened" by the COMMITTEE ON THE STATUS OF ENDANGERED WILDLIFE IN CANADA (COSEWIC), the Nisga'a Nation worried its connection to oolichan might also be in danger.

In 2013, after pushing for a re-assessment of oolichan as a "Species of Special Concern," the NISGA'A FISHERIES AND WILDLIFE DEPARTMENT undertook a multi-year research project that would provide concrete evidence of the fish's population, support its efforts at conserving the oolichan population, and ensure Nisga'a citizens can continue to harvest the fish each year.

A FISH CENTRAL TO NISGA'A CULTURE

The oolichan is a fish of many names: eulachon, ooligan, hooligan. It is sometimes called candlefish because it is so high in oil content that when dried it can be fitted with a wick and used as a candle. To scientists it is *Thaleichthys pacificus*. To the Nisga'a it is saak, or the saviour fish.

Every year in early spring, since before recorded time, Nisga'a have constructed camps along the banks of K̲'alii-Aksim Lisims (Nass River) to harvest and process oolichan. Lax- Da'oots'ip (Fishery Bay), where the glacial, blue waters of K̲'alii-Aksim Lisims meet the Pacific Ocean at Observatory Inlet, is the main harvesting centre for saak.

Historically, thousands of Nisga'a would spend months in Lax- Da'oots'ip, as they caught the first fish of the year. Nicole Morven, Harvest Monitoring Coordinator with Nisga'a Fisheries and Wildlife Department, recalls hearing from Elders that camps would operate for up to three months. "The women would be there too," she says. "Helping to get wood and clean up, getting the poles and gear ready for the whole season."

For us, it is a life-saving fish. It's the first fish that comes in the New Year arriving as winter supplies are dwindling.

The Nation has always held complete control over the area's oolichan run, providing them a source of wealth and power. "Of course there have been skirmishes back and forth over the years," says Harry Nyce Sr., director of the NISGA'A FISHERIES AND WILDLIFE DEPARTMENT. "But the Nisga'a were always successful according to our history."

Both the fish and the oil produced from processing it (t'ilx in Nisga'a) were valuable trading commodities between First Nations communities. Across the pacific northwest, "grease trails" formed where First Nations travelled, carrying their bentwood boxes of t'ilx for trade with other communities.

Although oolichan have always played a major role in the trading economies and culture of many First Nations, in Nisga'a territory the fish was never extensively exploited through Western commercial economies. Megan Moody, former Stewardship Director for the Nuxalk Nation, WRITES that a small commercial fishery for K'alii-Aksim Lisims oolichan existed in the first half of the 1900s until the Nisga'a Tribal Council Convention declared in 1955 that "no Nass River caught oolichans be sold commercially."

Today, most of the oolichan caught and processed on the Nass River are distributed among community members or traded with neighbouring First Nations. Saak and t'ilx continue to play a significant role in the economies of coastal communities as Nisga'a citizens trade their resource for shellfish, herring, seaweed, and halibut.

I can't ever imagine a day if they didn't come back.

Nyce, a hereditary chief whose Nisga'a name is Sim'oogit Naaws, says the fish continues to be a mainstay of Nisga'a culture. "For us, it is a life-saving fish," he says. "It's the first fish that comes in the New Year arriving as winter supplies are dwindling." HOOBIYEE, the Nisga'a new year, starts during spring equinox with the migration of saak into the K'alii-Aksim Lisims (Nass River).

Edward Desson, Fisheries Manager for the Nisga'a Fisheries and Wildlife Department, says there is a distinct energy in the Nass Valley when the oolichan start their spawning journey. "It's really hard to describe the buzz that goes on throughout the communities and how excited people get about the return of the oolichan," says Desson. "I can't ever imagine a day if they didn't come back."

For many First Nations however, that day has come.

Source: Nisga'a Nation. "The Saviour Fish: Protecting Nisga'a Connection to Oolichan." *Coast Funds*, coastfunds.ca/stories/the-saviour-fish-protecting-nisgaa-connection-to-oolichan/

Oolichan Grease

Near the end of each winter, the Nisga'a prepared for one of the most important fishing activities of the year: the annual oolichan run up the Nass River. Beginning around the end of February, they started to fish vast quantities of oolichan, a small and very oily member of the smelt family. One sign of the oolichans' arrival would be the sudden appearance of large numbers of sea mammals at the mouth of the river, as these animals hunted the oolichan.

Oolichan was not usually eaten as a fish meat. The vast majority of the catch was rendered for its edible grease which could be stored for many months. They boiled the oolichan in large cedar bent boxes until the grease separated and rose to the top. They then skimmed the grease and poured it into other boxes to store it for trade with other tribes or eating throughout the year. Oolichan contained so much grease that they could be burned like candles when dried, earning them the nickname "candlefish".

Oolichan Fishing

The Nisga'a traditionally fished oolichan with either nets or an oolichan rake called a k'idaa. The k'idaa was a long pole with comb-like wooden teeth on the end that was used to "rake" the oolichan from shallow areas of the river. For example, the ancient village of Ank'idaa took its name from the practice of catching oolichan with the k'idaa at that location.

Oolichan were also caught with nets. Sometimes a simple dip-net was used to scoop the oolichan out of the river, and other times a long oblong-shaped net would be anchored with tall stakes in the river and allowed to hang in the current. Every few minutes, the net would fill with oolichan and attendants would gather the net and empty it before setting it in the current again.

Dip-nets were made of twine spun from the fibrous pith of tall stinging nettles. The larger oblong-shaped net (called a "hlist") was made from twine that was spun from fireweed pith. The fireweed twine was known as "ẅahaas", or "thread-made-from-fire-weed".

Source: Government, Gingolx Village. "Oolichan Grease." *Ways of Life: Ancient Villages of the Nisga'a*, Apr. 2009, www.gingolx.ca/nisgaaculture/ancient_villages/way_of_life/grease.html.

About Samantha Beynon

Samantha Beynon is a mother of two. She was born and raised in Prince Rupert, British Columbia. She currently works and plays on the unceded territory of the Lekwungen and W̱SÁNEĆ peoples in Victoria British Columbia. She is mixed blood of Nisga'a, Tsimshian, Tlingit, Irish and Swedish. Samantha's Father is William Beynon the 4th, who is also mixed blood of Tsimshian, Nisga'a, Irish, and Swedish. William serves as an Aquatic Resource Manager for the Metlakatla Nation. His parents were Dora Adams from Aiyansh and William Beynon the 3rd from Lax Kw'alaams. Paternally she is the Great-Granddaughter of the Hereditary Chiefs William Beynon the 2nd and Chief Clah (Arthur Wellington).

Maternally, she comes from Wilps Axdii Wil Luugooda, The House that is Always Full in the Nass Valley. She is from the Ganhada/Frog clan and has maternal roots in Gingolx, British Columbia. Her grandparents are Jean (Trimble) Fitzgerald, and the late Brian Fitzgerald who comes from Irish ancestry from St John's, Newfoundland. Her Mother is Veronica Beynon (Trimble) who is mixed blood of Nisga'a and Irish. Samantha's Mother has always been her biggest role model throughout her life. Veronica benefits her local Indigenous community as an Indigenous Social Worker in Prince Rupert, British Columbia.

Growing up, Samantha was raised by her Mother, Father, Maternal Grandparents, Aunts and Uncles. Her and her maternal first cousins were raised extremely close. Traditionally, they did not think of themselves as 'first cousins' because they were raised as siblings. Despite living so far away, she remains extremely close to her family.

Samantha is very passionate about being the best educator for Indigenous and non-indigenous people. Both her maternal and paternal side both come from Northern Indigenous ancestry; therefore, it is very important to her to become the best role model for the future Indigenous generations. Being Indigenous, she feels Indigenous people may be able to connect and find a way to feel comfortable in their learning environments with her. Samantha believes with more Indigenous people becoming role models, Indigenous youth will have positive peers to look up to. Following the footsteps of her Great-Grandfather, author William Beynon 2nd, Samantha is hoping to make her ancestors proud. Through her books and education, her hopes are to help end vicious cycles and stereotypes surrounding historical abuses in Indigenous communities. Her passion is to help, guide and offer support to encourage successful experiences for all people to benefit from

About Lucy Trimble

Lucy Trimble waý, ii Hlgu Maksguum Ganaaw. Ksim Ganada ńiiý, ii Gingolx wil ẃitgwiý. Nisga'ahl nooý, ii Tlingithl nigwoodiý. Rose (Gurney)hl wahl agwii-nits'iits'iý, ii Christopher Trimblehl wahl agwii-niye'eý.

Lucy Trimble's traditional Nisga'a name is Hlgu Maksguum Ganaaw; she comes from Wilps Axdii Wil Luugooda, The House that is Always Full in the Nass Valley. She hails from the Frog clan and has maternal roots in Gingolx, British Columbia. Her Great Grandparents were the late Rose (Gurney) and late Christopher Trimble. Her Grandparents are Jean (Trimble) Fitzgerald, and the late Brian Fitzgerald. Her Mother is Carmelita Trimble, Father is John Heffernan and her Sister is Nakkita Trimble Wilson (along with all her sister cousins).

Paternally, she has a connection to Goulds, Newfoundland, with an Irish background. Lucy is currently an Indigenous Child and Youth Mental Health Clinician for coastal T'msyen communities and has been in the social service field for the past ten years. She holds an MSWI through the University of Victoria and is a student at the Freda Diesing School of Fine Art and Design. Her passion includes breathing life into land-based Indigenous ways of healing and seasonal traditional food harvesting.

Special thanks

Jean Fitzgerald (Trimble) – Samantha and
Lucy's Maternal Grandmother

William Beynon 4th – Metlakatla, Aquatic
Resource Manager– Samantha's Father

Wal·aks Keane Tait Nisga'a Language & Culture
Teacher – Samantha and Lucy's cousin

Brodie Guy – Coast Funds Chief Executive Officer

And special thanks to the Nisga'a Elders and
Knowledge Keepers surrounding the oolichan
fish that helped create this story.

Family Photos

Samantha's early traditional days

Samantha and her Maternal Grandmother Jean Fitzgerald

Samantha fishing with her parents at four years old on the Skenna River

Jean Fitzgerald with her Great-Granddaughter Rae Desautels

Jean Fitzgerald with her Great-Granddaughter Blake Desautels at her first birthday

Jean Fitzgerald

Brian Fitzgerald – Samantha's Maternal Grandfather

Samanth's Maternal Great-Grandmother Rose Trimble

Samantha's Great-Grandfather hereditary Tsimshian Chief William Beynon 2nd

32

Samantha's Paternal Grandparents and Father

Samantha's 3rd Great-Grandfather Arthur Wellington – Chief Clah

Samantha's parents with her daughters Rae and Blake

Wilfred Langdon Kihn and William Beynon, salmon fishing, Gitkinlkul (Gitanyow), British Columbia, 1924.

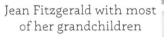

Jean Fitzgerald with most of her grandchildren

Samantha with her Daughters, Rae and Blake

33

Works Cited

First Peoples' Cultural Council (FPCC). "Nisga'a."
    FirstVoices, 10 Feb. 2021, www.firstvoices.com/
    explore/FV/sections/Data/Nisga'a/Nisga'a/Nisga'a.

Government, Gingolx Village. "Oolichan Grease." *Ways of Life:
    Ancient Villages of the Nisga'a*, Apr. 2009, www.gingolx.
    ca/nisgaaculture/ancient_villages/way_of_life/grease.html.

Nisga'a Nation. "The Saviour Fish: Protecting
    Nisga'a Connection to Oolichan."
    Coast Funds, coastfunds.ca/stories/
    the-saviour-fish-protecting-nisgaa-connection-to-oolichan/

PICTURES

Canadian Museum of History, "William Beynon." *Gateway
    to Aboriginal Heritage*, n.d., https://www.historymuseum.
    ca/cmc/exhibitions/tresors/ethno/etp1100e.html -

"Arthur Willington Clah." *Wikipedia*, last updated
    24 Nov. 2020, 16:05 UTC, https://en.wikipedia.
    org/wiki/Arthur_Wellington_Clah

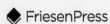 FriesenPress

Suite 300 - 990 Fort St
Victoria, BC, V8V 3K2
Canada

www.friesenpress.com

Illustrated by Lucy Trimble

Michelle Stoney - Artist with the two little black and white girls holding hands on the cover

ISBN
978-1-03-910388-7 (Hardcover)
978-1-03-910387-0 (Paperback)
978-1-03-910389-4 (eBook)

1. Juvenile Fiction, People & Places, Canada, Native Canadian

Distributed to the trade by The Ingram Book Company